Margot Moose

Summertime Sensations

Sarah Ventura-Wright

Tellwell Talent
www.tellwell.ca

ISBN
978-0-2288-8067-7 (Hardcover)
978-0-2288-8066-0 (Paperback)

About the Author:

Sarah Ventura-Wright was born and raised in Chatham, Ontario. She is a wife and a mother to two amazing children. Bringing awareness to Sensory Processing Disorder is extremely important to her and what inspires her writing.

Dedication:

To my wonderful husband Joe and my two beautiful children Lennox and Leticia- without you three this book would not have been possible. Your love and support has pushed me to pursue dreams I never thought possible. I love you! #dreamteam #squadgoals

It was a lovely hot summer day. Margot the moose and her best friends Sutton the squirrel and Boden the beaver pack up for a fun day at the beach. When they arrive, Margot the moose seemed unhappy. Boden the beaver said, "Margot, what's wrong? You seem upset." Margot replied, "the bright sun is really bothering me. It's hurting my head and I can't open my eyes."

Sutton the squirrel quickly opens up the beach bag and pulls out a pair of sunglasses. "Here you go Margot. If you put these sunglasses on they will help you block out the bright light from the sun." Margot the moose put on the pretty purple sunglasses and looked around. She looked to her left and then to her right. A big smile spread across her face. "Thank you Sutton! These sunglasses are so helpful. My headache is disappearing. I can see the white powdered sand and crystal clear water now."

Together the three friends continued to walk together towards the water. "Ouch, ouch ouch," Margot the moose shouted while jumping up and down on the white powdered sand with her bare feet. "Margot, what's wrong? Are you hurt?" asked Boden the beaver. Margot shouted, "the sand is too hot and it's hurting my feet."

Sutton the squirrel quickly opens up the beach bag and pulls out a pair of water shoes. "Here you go Margot. If you put on these water shoes they will help you walk on the sand easily." Margot the moose put on the cherry red water shoes. She took one step and then two more. A big smile spread across her face. "Thank you Sutton! These water shoes are so helpful. I can walk on the sand and it does not hurt my feet anymore."

Together the three friends continue to make their way to the water. They find the perfect spot to set up their beach umbrellas, chairs and towels. The crashing of the waves along the shoreline mesmerizes them all.

Margot the moose starts to move around in her chair and cup her ears with her hands. Boden the beaver says, "Margot, what's wrong? You seem uncomfortable." Margot replied, "the sounds of the waves are very loud and it's causing a ringing sound in my ears."

Sutton the squirrel quickly opens up the beach bag and pulls out a pair of bright orange swimming earplugs. "Here you go Margot. If you put these swimming earplugs in they will block out the sounds of the waves." Margot the moose put in the left earplug and then the right. She could barely hear the waves anymore. A big smile spread across her face. "Thank you Sutton. These swimming earplugs are so helpful. I can hardly hear the waves anymore and the ringing sound has disappeared." Margot the moose, Boden the beaver and Sutton the squirrel built sandcastles together, jumped over the waves and collected seashells along the shoreline. They had a delightful day relishing in all of the beaches summertime sensations.

Made in the USA
Monee, IL
28 November 2022